For
Ezra & Raphael.

Two radical turtles!
Always follow your
hearts

Jaimal Yogis

Turtles Don't Surf

Turtles Don't Surf

Print production and book design by:
RelKeyBooks.com, Folsom, California

Printed and bound in Shanghai, China

First Printing, 2013

ISBN: 978-0-9897321-0-9

Pelagic Books
2526 Great Highway
San Francisco, CA. 94116

To order books or need information contact us at:
www.jaimalyogis.com

The wind whirred. The waves boomed. And little Kai
the sea turtle was stuck in his room: grounded.

Kai had been trying to break the sacred code, the one that every ocean animal knows: Turtles can glide. Turtles can float. Turtles can cruise like a glass-bottomed boat. But search the Bahamas. Search the whole earth. Search every island -- TURTLES DON'T SURF!

But Kai couldn't help it. He fantasized. He schemed.
He'd seen dolphins and pelicans and seals on the scene.
And he vowed to himself: someday that will be me!

Only each time Kai tried, he felt like a faker. Try as he might, he couldn't paddle out past the breakers. A show-offey dolphin cut him off in a burst. "Hey Kai," said the dolphin, "TURTLES DON'T SURF!"

And as if things couldn't get any worse, mom and dad caught him, flustered and terse. "We've told you 100 times, Kai, we've told you since birth. You mustn't disobey. TURTLES DON'T SURF."
"But Mom," Kai pleaded, "there has to be a first!"

Kai's parents tried to hide their pride. But honestly, how could they let this slide? It would be all over the Starfish Star News – "Turtle thinks he can shoot the tube." For Kai's own good, they had to lock him tight in his room.

That night the surf lulled Kai to sleep, and he met
a dream octopus with eight arms and eight feet.

Imagining the octopus had him in tow, Kai found
himself sleep paddling out the window.

The currents carried Kai to the far off reaches…

...and he woke up yawning on the most curious of beaches. The strangest sign stood firm in the earth, a message written in red: DOLPHINS DON'T SURF! And out on the break, with hoots and high fives, turtles were getting the rides of their lives.

"Halejua!" Kai laughed out loud. "A land of turtle surfers. This is my crowd." And now that he knew a turtle could do it, Kai went straight for the foam — and paddled right through it! "So it's easy as that," Kai said to the sea. "To do something difficult, you have to believe."

"That's right," said a voice from inside a wave. A turtle emerged, saying – "hey bro, I'm Dave." "I can see that you're new," Dave said with a laugh. "I can tell by your do. But it's cool, man, relax. As I tell all my bros, as I always say, every turtle can surf. It's our nature to play."

Dave taught Kai to surf like only a turtle can dare: 360 shell spinners, and the four-fin spread air, the no-look tube ride and the side shell cutter. "You're a natural," said Dave. "I've never seen better. There's only one thing to do. I've done what I can. It's time to send you the…

"Turtle Pro-Am!"

"We'll set you up in a blue whale Westfalia! And away you'll go to western Australia, to the Tortuga Annual in southern Chile, and the Turtle World Classic in tropical Tahiti. Kai – welcome to your new family!" said Dave.

Kai gulped: should he go with the pros, looking so cool with their toes on the nose? The blue whale Westfalia, that could be nice. But then Kai saw something he really didn't like.

Out in the breakers, he heard huff, then a puff, a grr,
then a whimper, a hrumphheeee-PTUFF! A small spinner
dolphin fighting for all she was worth, while the turtle
pros heckled: DOLPHINS DON'T SURF!"

The pros asked Kai to join, but he didn't like this one morsel.
He knew what it was like to be on the flip side of that dorsal.
Kai swam to the dolphin to help her out of the rip. "Hi!" said
the dolphin. "My name is Flip!"

"Thanks for the lessons," Kai said to Dave.
"Flip, I'll show you a better wave."
So Kai and Flip swam down into darkness,
searching for that dream octopus.

The octopus opened a doorway home, where Kai's family was
crying on the conch telephone. "Have you seen our son, Kai?"
they cried and they moaned.

"I'm right here," Kai shouted, filled with elation.
"And I swear, I have an explanation! Hermit
crabs and eels, every urchin on the reef, residents
of the ocean, I'm going to make a speech!"

The animals gathered in a raucous herd. But Kai said nothing,
not one word. He paddled through the breakers and planting a
fin, Kai simply dropped right in. Shredding in loops and twists on
the face, he carved "TURTLES CAN SURF" right into the wave!

"Kai," said the dolphins, "you've taught us a lesson."
And out they swam for an all-animal surf session.
And this time since Flip saw that dolphins could do it,
she dove into the foam and paddled right through it.

The sun shone brighter. A breeze blew over the sea. The oysters and clams sang a sweet Tweedledeedeee. And in a moment of clarity, every ocean critter could see: If you want to do something difficult, you have to believe.

Jaimal Yogis is the author of two internationally-acclaimed surfing memoirs, Saltwater Buddha (currently being made into a feature-length film) and The Fear Project. His award-winning writing has also been published in The Washington Post, The Surfer's Journal, ESPN Magazine, and many others. Jaimal wrote and illustrated Turtles Can Surf, his first children's book, while awaiting the birth of his first son, Kaifas (Kai for short). Jaimal and his family live across the street from San Francisco's Ocean Beach where Kai is becoming increasingly brazen in the icy waves. For more information on other books by Jaimal, go to www.jaimalyogis.com